Kiki
My Stylish Life

READ ALL THE
LOTUS LANE BOOKS!

LOTUS LANE

Kiki

My
Stylish
Life

by Kyla May

BRANCHES™

SCHOLASTIC INC.

To my wonderful sister, Amber,
and to Holmwood Avenue—
the best street to grow up on.

Library of Congress Cataloging-in-Publication Data
May, Kyla. Kiki: my stylish life / by Kyla May.
p. cm. — (Lotus Lane ; 1)
Summary: Kiki and her best friends, Coco and Lulu, all live on Lotus Lane, attend Amber Acres Elementary School, and have their own club, so when a when a Japanese girl named Mika moves in next door and also chooses fashion design for her art project, Kiki is seriously annoyed.
ISBN 978-0-545-44512-2 (pbk.)—ISBN 978-0-545-49613-1 (hardback)—ISBN 978-0-545-49680-3 (ebook)
1. Fashion design—Juvenile fiction. 2. Best friends—Juvenile fiction. 3. Friendship—Juvenile fiction. 4. Popularity—Juvenile fiction. 5. Elementary schools—Juvenile fiction. 6. Diary fiction. [1. Fashion—Fiction. 2. Best friends—Fiction. 3. Friendship—Fiction. 4. Popularity—Fiction. 5. Elementary schools—Fiction. 6. Schools—Fiction. 7. Diaries—Fiction.] I. Title. II. Title: My stylish life.
PZ7.M4535Kik 2013
813.6—dc23
2012034246

ISBN 978-0-545-49613-1 (hardcover) / ISBN 978-0-545-44512-2 (paperback)

25 24 23 22 21   20 21 22 23 24/0

Printed in China
First Scholastic printing, May 2013

TABLE OF CONTENTS

THIS
DIARY
BELONGS TO
Kiki

Chapter 1

Kiki

All About Me

Thursday

~~Hello~~ ... ~~Hi Diary~~ ...?
~~Welcome~~ ... Ta daaa!
I'd like to introduce myself.
I am Kiki, World-Famous **Style Star**!

Okay, that's way **OTT**!
It's not like I'm on the red
carpet ... <u>yet</u>! (Sorry, this
whole writing-in-a-diary business
is totally new to me.)

OTT =
over the
top

Starting over ...

1

Dear Diary,

My name is Kiki Louise Keenan. I am a puppy dog owner and a triple chicken owner. I am also the 3rd oldest in my family (after Mom and Dad).

And I absolutely LOVE to collect facts.

 I will one day be a VERY famous fashion designer.

 I am quite the worrier.

 I am a member of the Lotus Lane Girls Club (**LLGC** for short).

Let me explain more
about the LLGC...
I'm the lifetime **BFF**
of Coco Corvino and Lulu Lyons,
my fellow Lotus Lane Girls.
We set up the LLGC so we could
spend ALL our time together.

We all live on Lotus Lane, the prettiest street in **Amber Acres**.

Coco's house

Lulu's house

LOTUS LANE

Each week we have fun LLGC activities:

	MONDAY	TUESDAY	WEDNESDAY
Club Name	Super Scrapbooking	Doggie Day Spa	Ten-Minute Makeover
Club Activity	Create scrapbook pages	Pamper our pets	Do manicures pedicures, and style our hair
Club Location	Kiki's house	Coco's backyard	Lulu's bedroom

LOTUS LANE GIRLS CLUB SCHEDULE

THURSDAY	FRIDAY	SATURDAY	SUNDAY
LOTUS DAY OFF	Pajama Party	Cupcake Catch-Up	LOTUS DAY OFF
	Watch movies, eat popcorn, gossip	Bake cupcakes	
	Kiki's, Lulu's, or Coco's house	Coco's kitchen	

Getting back to **YOU**, Diary.

Mom surprised me first thing this morning with . . . you! Mom travels lots for work. She gave me you so I can write down everything that happens in my super-stylish life while she's away. Mom's away <u>next</u> week so I better get the hang of this diary thing. I write about what's happening right now in my life, right?

Tomorrow's Funky Fashion Friday and we can wear whatever we like to school. Given the style star that I am, I must look 100% awesome! (P.S. I go to Amber Acres Elementary School.)

Okay, Maxi, let's get fashion-focused.
Oops, I haven't yet told you about

Maxi!

He is my dog. He is
the cutest dog in
Amber Acres, and
possibly the world.

Maxi usually helps me choose outfits. But right
now he is NOT being helpful at all!!!

FACT — Maxi is <u>NOT</u> the
best-behaved dog in
Amber Acres!

**Look at him hiding
clothes under my bed!**

9

For Funky Fashion Friday, how about this outfit?

Or this?

Or this?

EEK! It's late, so I'd better get to sleep. The chosen outfit will have to wait till the morning.

Good night, Diary. (z z Z Z)

Chapter 2

Friday

Oh no, Diary! I had the worst nightmare last night! It was terrible!!!!! And now it's for real. . . . I don't know what to wear for Funky Fashion Friday.

Thank goodness my BFFs are just a text away. Coco and Lulu will save me!

Kiki: Help! What r u wearing 2day?

Coco: Not a clue.

Lulu: You 2 r just deciding now!!!!?!

Kiki: Should i wear this?

#1

Kiki: Or this?

#2

Coco: Both...Hmm, either? I don't know...? :) 🧁 ♥

Lulu: I <3 #2. Gorgeous!!!
c u @ skl
ps Make sure u wear yr hair up. With side sweep @ front. 🌸 👓

FACT Lulu had her Funky Fashion Friday outfit picked out weeks ago.

Looks like option #2 is the way to go.
Nightmare over. Phew!

I'm so lucky to have such AWESOME
BFFLs. Wait a minute, Diary, I
haven't told you much about the
other LLGC members, have I?

BFFL=
best friend
for life

the land of pizza & pasta
Italy

Coco

Evie,
her dog

This is Coco. She lives at #6 [LOTUS LANE] and she's
the best cook I know. And she's a great baker,
too. Her parents come from Italy . . . her
whole family is totally obsessed with pasta!

Here's Lulu. She lives
at #8 LOTUS LANE.
Lulu's life = saving money
and planning her future.
She says things like
"The future is now." Or
"Don't dream it, do it."

Oh, and she's half French because
her dad is from France. How cool
is that?!

Bosco, her cat, who thinks he is a dog

Oh no, look at the time!!!!!
I'd better get dressed for
Funky Fashion Friday.

Catch ya after school.

WOW—what a day!!!!!! My outfit was a total (um, of course) hit! Lulu's outfit looked really cool, too. And Coco, well, let's just say she doesn't ♥ fashion as much as we do.

LLGC PAJAMA PARTY CHECKLIST

☑ Sleuth Sally DVD

☑ Popcorn

Must dash! The Lotus Lane Girls will be here any second for our LLGC Pajama Party. It's at my house this week. Sleuth Sally is the theme of tonight's sleepover!! Lulu's bringing the popcorn. Coco's bringing the movie **Sleuth Sally & the Secret Stairway**, starring Penelope Glitter. This movie is #1 on our top ten best-movies-of-all-time list.

FACT

Coco, Lulu, and I absolutely LOVE Sleuth Sally!

i ♥ SLEUTH SALLY

Sleuth Sally solves magical mysteries, leaving a trail of glitter behind her. How cool is that? Lulu says LLGC should open a detective agency just like Sleuth Sally's one day.

Must go—loads to do. **Ciao**!

CIAO =
Italian for "hi" and "bye"

P.S. Check out how much sleepover prep I've already done!

Pass the Snooze Button, Please

Saturday

Lulu, Coco, and I stayed up talking till midnight.

FACT

LLGC up talking till midnight = unhappy parents.

I'm SO tired today! I made it downstairs to have a yummy oatmeal breakfast with Lulu and Coco before they headed home. Then I rolled right back into bed. . . .

Mom just came in to tell me to hurry up and get dressed. But I have NOTHING to wear. Zilch. I've worn everything cool at least once! I tried to tell Mom that, but she just called back:

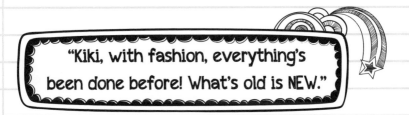

"Kiki, with fashion, everything's been done before! What's old is NEW."

19

Mom must be right because she knows fashion better than anyone I know. She's a <u>REAL-LIFE</u> Fashion Stylist. That means her job is to dress people for fashion shows and events. So Mom is the best person ever to shop with—especially when it comes to **vintage** clothes shopping!

VINTAGE = a fancy way of saying "old"

Check out the vintage clothes Mom and I found last week:

1960s hat

1980s sweater

1970s scarf

1930s hairclip

1930s pants

clutch

clogs

Hmmm. Today, maybe I could wear this scarf as a belt . . . ?

And add this skirt as a top?

And then maybe add this hairclip as a pin?

I must text Lulu my outfit. She'll love it.

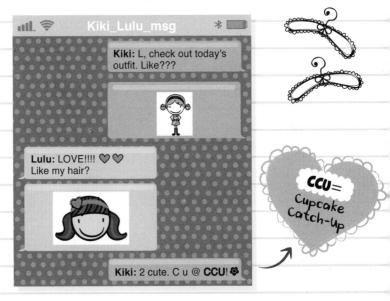

Kiki_Lulu_msg

Kiki: L, check out today's outfit. Like???

Lulu: LOVE!!!! ♡ ♡ Like my hair?

Kiki: 2 cute. C u @ **CCU**! ☺

CCU = Cupcake Catch-Up

Okay, I'm heading downstairs to start my day now. . . .

Diary, I must tell you something I forgot to fill you in on yesterday! You see, yesterday in art class we were given a new art project. Miss Melody (my favorite teacher in the whole world!) asked us to choose an area of art that we're really "passionate" about (which it turns out means choosing something we're really interested in, and has nothing to do with passion fruit).

On Tuesday, we will have to tell Miss Melody which type of art we'll do for the project.

I ♥ FASHION

Last night at our LLGC Pajama Party, Coco, Lulu, and I picked our art passions. Lulu chose pottery (because she plans to start selling vases).

FACT Lulu is always coming up with money-making ideas.

Coco chose painting (because the most famous painters in history are Italian—just like her).

And I chose fashion design. Of course!!

My project will be to design 4 outfits in 12 days (EEK!). I'll present my designs in a fashion parade during school assembly, and Lulu and Coco have offered to be my models. Lulu's and Coco's art will also be on display that day. Oh, and prizes will be awarded. I want to win one!!

This project is the best!

Must run to Coco's house for our Cupcake
Catch-Up! Today we're making my all-time
favorite cupcake flavor—
Raspberry with Vanilla Frosting.
Beyond **delish**! Bye!

DELISH=
fun way of
saying
"delicious"

MY TOP 5 CUPCAKE FLAVORS

1. Raspberry with Vanilla Frosting

2. Cherry and Chocolate Delight

3. Double Chocolate Chip with
   Pink Frosting

4. Cherry and Coconut Bliss

5. Strawberry with Raspberry
   Frosting

Chapter 4

Sunday

BIG NEWS: A new family is moving in next door! Sweet... I'm SO excited to meet them!

Hmmm... I must do some Sleuth Sally investigating! So far this morning I've seen the following items delivered next door:

• A super-cute dollhouse ⟹

- An awesome bike with glitter streamers

- A pink Sleuth Sally guitar

My expert mystery-solving skills tell me there must be a girl my age moving in! I wonder if I'll like her. I wonder if Coco and Lulu will like her.

I think someone's at our front door because Maxi is barking like crazy. Have to go!

No one was at the door, but I think I just saw a REAL pony going into the new neighbors' house! A pony on Lotus Lane!?!

Last year, I begged Mom and Dad for a pony, but instead I got 3 chickens: Henny, Penny, and Brian. When Brian was little, we thought he was a boy. But it turns out he's a <u>she</u> (which I'm sure is confusing for Brian!).

CLUCK
CLUCK

FACT   Even chickens must look their best.

Henny, Penny, and Brian lay lots of eggs so we eat lots of eggs: scrambled eggs, poached eggs, fried eggs . . .

FACT   Eggs aren't so yummy when you have them <u>ALL</u> the time.

Mom wants me to go say hello to the new neighbors . . . and to take them some eggs! Really . . . eggs?! I better run!

My house   Neighbor's house

Okay, no one answered so I left the eggs on their doorstep. There were lots of boxes on the porch. What if the boxes fall and crush the eggs? What if the pony gets scared by the falling boxes and jumps the fence, crushes Mom's flowers, and . . . urggggh! Okay, need to stop stressing! (See? I'm such a worrier!)

What!!!!?!! There's now a truck full of sand next door! Huh???? I can see a girl my age standing in the backyard, too. She looks cool. I love her clothes. Her skirt is super cute. And that top— it's gorgeous.

But back to the sand . . . why so much sand? Are they making a beach in their backyard? I do love the beach!

Are they building a pyramid?

Maybe they have giant pet ants?

Hi! Hello! Howdy! Good morning!

Or maybe they are building a huge sand castle for when mermaid royalty comes to visit?

Let's hope it's a beach. How awesome!?! LLGC could go surfing whenever we wanted! Well, I guess water would need to be delivered for that to work. . . . I'll keep you posted, Diary! I can't wait to tell Lulu and Coco about the sand tomorrow at school! **TTYL**!

TTYL= talk to you later

Chapter 5

LOL.
Not!

LOL= laugh out loud

Monday

DISASTER!

Rewind... Yesterday afternoon, I had the best idea EVER! I decided to take some fresh-baked cupcakes to the new neighbors (from Saturday's Cupcake Catch-Up)! Why didn't I think of that <u>before</u> giving eggs to the neighbors? EGGS?! If there <u>could</u> be a new LLGC member next door, I had to give her my very best welcome possible.

Anyhow,
I boxed up
some Raspberry Vanilla cupcakes,
but on my way next door,
I accidentally left our front gate open!

OOPSY.

Maxi raced out and ran straight into the new neighbors' backyard. He started digging up all that sand and making a <u>HUGE</u> mess!

Then the neighbors' dog (who is NOT a pony by the way but <u>is</u> the biggest dog I've ever seen!) started barking at Maxi. I ran over as quickly as I could.

Well, that girl in the cool clothes was there. She looked really pretty—but also really, <u>REALLY</u> unhappy. It turns out her name is Mika.

The sand is part of her family's very special "Zen garden." Mika's family just moved here from Japan. She said they were building the Zen garden because they had wanted to bring something special from Japan with them to their new home.

I felt so badly and I said  a million times.

I'm sorry. I'm sorry. I'm sorry. I'm sorry. I'm sorry.
I'm sorry. I'm sorry. I'm sorry. I'm sorry. I'm sorry.
I'm sorry. I'm sorry. I'm sorry. I'm sorry. I'm sorry.
I'm sorry. I'm sorry. I'm sorry. I'm sorry. I'm sorry.
I'm sorry. I'm sorry. I'm sorry. I'm sorry. I'm sorry.
I'm sorry. I'm sorry. I'm sorry. I'm sorry. I'm sorry.
I'm sorry. I'm sorry. I'm sorry. I'm sorry. I'm sorry.
I'm sorry. I'm sorry. I'm sorry. I'm sorry. I'm sorry.
I'm sorry. I'm sorry. I'm sorry. I'm sorry. I'm sorry.
I'm sorry. I'm sorry. I'm sorry. I'm sorry. I'm sorry.
I'm sorry. I'm sorry. I'm sorry. I'm sorry. I'm sorry.
I'm sorry. I'm sorry. I'm sorry. I'm sorry. I'm sorry.
I'm sorry. I'm sorry. I'm sorry. I'm sorry. I'm sorry.
I'm sorry. I'm sorry. I'm sorry. I'm sorry. I'm sorry.
I'm sorry. I'm sorry. I'm sorry. I'm sorry. I'm sorry.
I'm sorry. I'm sorry. I'm sorry. I'm sorry. I'm sorry.

And I said that Maxi didn't mean it. Then
I tried to make Mika laugh by saying,
"Maybe I should have brought a shovel with
me instead of cupcakes." *(hehe)* Mika didn't laugh.
Instead she said, "Next time your dog
comes into my yard, I'm calling
the dogcatcher!"

I felt totally upset. I shoved the cupcakes at her and ran home. Meanie! Maxi didn't know any better. Double Meanie. With sand on top!

Mom says it's hard moving to a new place — especially from as far away as Japan. She's sure Mika didn't mean what she said about the dogcatcher.

VERY FAR away

Mika's new house

YEAH . . . RİGHT!

Mika:

Sand sculptor ➡ NO!
Ant Collector ➡ NO!
Surfer ➡ NO!
New BFF & Future Lotus Lane
Girls Club member
➡ definitely NOT!!!!!

That all happened yesterday. But just wait, Diary, because today things got even worse...

Guess what? Not only does Mika go to my school, she's in MY class!

In between math and social studies, I filled Coco and Lulu in on all the drama. They can't believe how mean Mika is. Coco said during recess Mika even pointed at me while talking to Katy Krupski (the school's Queen of Mean)!! I bet they are already BFFs. That would make complete sense.

Katy Krupski

Mika Maeda

I asked Miss Melody about Zen gardens, and she lent me a book about Japan.

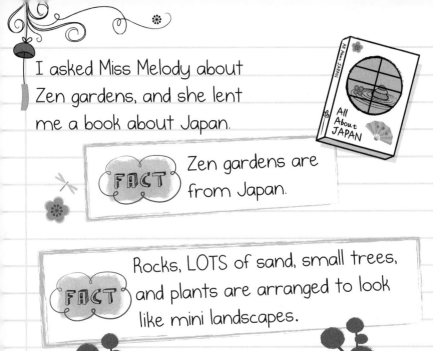

FACT Zen gardens are from Japan.

FACT Rocks, LOTS of sand, small trees, and plants are arranged to look like mini landscapes.

FACT Sand represents water. You rake the sand into wave shapes so it looks like the sea or a river.

(No swimsuit needed.)

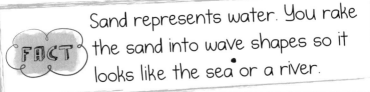

FACT "Zen" means peaceful.

FACT Maxi is NOT Zen.

Zen gardens actually look pretty amazing. In fact, I am making them the theme for Super Scrapbooking tonight.

BTW, I'm excited for tomorrow—I can't wait to tell Miss Melody that I've chosen fashion for the BIG art project! It's going to be great! Okay, Lulu and Coco are coming over so I better run.
Till tomorrow.

BTW = by the way

Chapter 6

I Worry Because I Can

Tuesday

Being a style star, I like to change outfits throughout the day to match my mood. Doesn't every fashion superstar? I'm in the mood for navy blue. Maybe a dress? One of my favorite all-time supermodels wore lots of cute dresses. Her name was **Twiggy**.

TWIGGY = British fashion model from the 1960s

Twiggy wore dresses just like this ➡

I'll write more after school!

Today in art class, my art project plan was TOTALLY ruined—all because of Meanie Mika! She chose fashion for her art passion—just like me!! COPYCAT!

cat copycat

And I bet Mika's really good at coming up with fashion designs. Her outfit today was even better than yesterday.

MIKA'S OUTFIT TODAY ➡

i ♥ her heart-shaped handbag

Mika choosing fashion too has really thrown me.
I have no idea what to do for my designs. Mom
always says:

> **"To be creative, you first
> must be inspired."**

That Japanese book inspired my
scrapbooking last night.... Could it inspire my
fashion designs, too? I'll have to read more of
it later tonight.

the scrapbooking i did last night

Right now, I must get to Doggie
Day Spa at Coco's house.
I'm definitely putting the
leash on Maxi.... I do
not want him to end up at
the dogcatcher!!

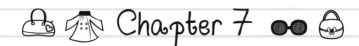

Chapter 7

I ♥ Coco

Wednesday

Maxi

Bosco

Evie

Doggie Day Spa was soooo much fun yesterday! Did I mention that the LLGC meets every week with our pets and we treat our four-legged BFFs like royalty? This happens at Coco's house. (She loves animals!)

How do you like Maxi's new look? It was Coco's idea to add the polka-dotted bows!

Bosco, the cat-dog

Diary, this is Bosco. Yes, you are right, he is not a dog. He is Lulu's cat. But he totally thinks he's a dog so he comes to Doggie Day Spa. He even fetches sticks!

This morning, Mom woke me up SUPER early. She has to go away for one whole week. That's seven entire days!! Drat. I really wanted her help with my art project! AND she'll miss my fashion parade next Wednesday!!! ☹

Mom

I miss her SO much (times 50 million) already, and it hasn't even been one day. But when Mom's away, Dad does let me watch TV past bedtime. And when Mom comes home, she brings the best-ever presents.

Last time, I got a beret (SAY: bear-ray), which sounds like a bear that looks like a stingray. But it's actually a hat from France.

Good thing Mom gave me you, Diary, so I can remember to tell her everything she misses. Did I tell you that now Coco and Lulu want diaries, too?!

Today at school, Miss Melody brought in heaps of fabrics for the fashion students to use. We were each told to choose two fabrics. I chose a cherry blossom fabric and one with fans on it.

Surprise, surprise . . . Mika chose <u>EXACTLY</u> the same fabrics! (Double copycat!) How can I be a unique designer with Mika copying everything I do?!?!

Oh! It's time for Ten-Minute Makeover at Lulu's house. Lulu loves hairstyles and movie stars. And she has more magazines than anyone I know. Today she's sharing her latest mag with us—gotta go!!

At Ten-Minute Makeover, we spent 10 minutes doing hair and over an hour chatting about Mika. BTW, check out Lulu's latest hairdo! Stunning, isn't it?

LULU'S NEW HAIRDO

Lulu and Coco have such awesome hair. I wish I had Lulu's hair. But Lulu wants my hair. I guess Mom's saying is true:

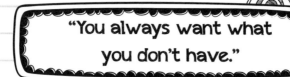

"You always want what you don't have."

I'm so lucky to have Coco and Lulu helping me through this Mika drama. This is what they had to say after art class today . . .

"Mika shouldn't have chosen the same fabrics as you." — **Lulu**

"It's SO obvious she's trying to outdo you, Kiki." — **Coco**

"Yeah, even if she wanted those fabrics, you chose first so she should have chosen different ones." — **Lulu**

We all agree that what Mika did today was

JUST. NOT. COOL.

Chapter 8

Fabulousness Is Hard Work

Thursday

Look at my outfit.
I'm a total mess.

I'm SOOOOO stressed about
the fashion parade next week!
Tomorrow we have to present our
design drawings in class. **EEK!** I for sure have
designer's block—I don't have a clue what to
draw! Hold on. My phone just beeped.
Mom texted me from Milan!

Mom: How R U Kiki-kins? Miss U darling. Here's what i did 2day. What r u up 2? R U ok? XxX 💙

Kiki: Hi Mom. So stressed! Need 2 show fashion designs in art 2moro. Can't come up with anything. ☹

Mom: There's a box in my closet behind my skirts. Find it . . . it will inspire you. Don't stress. You are so creative. XxX💙🧁

Kiki: 4 real????!!!! Thx Mom! U R the best! Love U XXXXXOOOOO 💙 💙 💙

Mom: Good luck, angel! Love u XxX 💙

This calls for an LLGC Emergency Meeting.

Kiki: LLGC Emergency meeting: My place **ASAP**! Love, Kiki ♡ ♡ ♡

ASAP= as soon as possible

Yay... I'm so excited to open that box! WOW, I'm usually never <u>EVER</u> allowed in Mom's closet!!! I can't wait for the girls to get here. Ohhh, I just heard the doorbell... more later!!

Coco, Lulu, and I opened the box. Oh my!!!!! It was incredible. We found tons of Japanese kimonos inside made out of really amazing materials. (I recognized the kimonos from Miss Melody's book about Japan!)

FACT A kimono is a traditional Japanese robe worn by men, women, and children.

kimono

FACT Even sumo wrestlers wear kimonos.

FACT A kimono is shaped like the letter T and has big sleeves.

FACT A kimono is wrapped around the body. The left side always wraps over the right (just like my bathrobe!).

FACT A kimono is tied with a sash called an "obi."

FACT I am 100% inspired by Mom's kimonos!

Coco and Lulu helped me brainstorm awesome design drawing ideas.
No more designer's block for me!
HOOOOOOOORRRAAY!

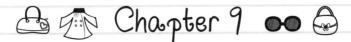

Chapter 9

So Far, So Bad

Milan, ITALY

Friday

Today I am going to wear something Italian because Mom is in Milan, Italy. Milan is one of the fashion capitals of the world! I'll write more tonight. TTYL! CIAO!

Oh my . . . what should have been a great day turned out not-so-great! I went to art class all ready to share my design drawings from last night. But Mika asked to go first. Miss Melody let her. (She doesn't know any better.) Everyone absolutely ADORED Mika's drawings, which would have been fine EXCEPT her designs look almost <u>exactly</u> like mine . . . only better!!

Coco and Lulu couldn't believe it either. Here's what they said at lunch (almost word for word):

"Mika totally copied you, Kiki! She must have spies!" — Coco

"Yeah! She must be your enemy. Just like Sleuth Sally's enemy, Dull Dastardly!" — Lulu

Lulu can get carried away, but maybe she's right on this one.

Mika's design

My design

FACT Mika Maeda is trouble!

After class, I told Miss Melody that I thought Mika was a copycat.

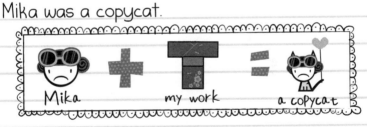

Mika + my work = a copycat

Miss Melody brought Mika over so we could "talk things out." Ugh. Why do teachers do that?! Mika said, "Kiki is the one copying! When she came to my house, she must have seen our family kimono hanging on the wall!"

I said, "I haven't even been <u>inside</u> Mika's house! Coco and Lulu helped me come up with this idea yesterday."

Miss Melody asked us to calm down. But Mika butted in, "My grandma, who is also from Japan, knows all there is to know about kimonos. She helped ME come up with this idea WAY before yesterday!"

Miss Melody said Mika and I are "simply on the same creative page" and that clearly there was no copycat at work. We are most definitely <u>NOT</u> on the same ANYTHING! I'm nothing like Mika. I'm on my OWN page.

My page

Mika's page

And then my day got even worse! Miss Melody said she wants Mika and me to work TOGETHER on a banner for the fashion parade during recess on Monday. NOT FAIR!!!!!!!

Thank goodness tonight is our LLGC Pajama Party. I SO need some time to chill with my Lotus Lane Girls. The sleepover is at Lulu's house and the theme is All Things French. Lulu's dad just got back from France with yummy treats . . .
I can't wait!

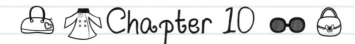

Chapter 10

Sweet Cherry Blossoms

Saturday

Last night's sleepover was SO fun! We all put on berets and pretended we were visiting France. For dessert, Lulu's dad made croissants and we ate strawberries —YUM!

croissant

FACT Lulu's dad is a much better cook than my dad.

We watched the movie **Sleuth Sally in Paris**, where someone in France pretends to be Sally and gives her a bad name. After the movie, Lulu said something that totally freaked me out:

" maybe mika wants to pretend she's YOU just like Sally's evil-doing double!" — Lulu

Like I said, Lulu can get carried away sometimes. But . . . wait a minute. Maybe Lulu's right! What if Mika does want to be me? I mean, Miss Melody did say we were on the same creative page, and Mika does have a great sense of fashion, and she does live on Lotus Lane. Maybe she'll even start living in my house and Mom and Dad won't know she's not me! (Sleuth Sally's Mom didn't realize Sally's double wasn't Sally!)
Oh no!!

But then this morning I realized I was just being silly. Sleuth Sally movies make our imaginations run wild!

last night

now

Lulu's dad made French toast with orange slices for breakfast. That sure helped clear my mind!

FACT French toast = beyond delish!

So I've been home for a while trying to work on turning my design drawings into actual clothing. Hmmm . . . my sewing machine is totally

confusing me. But I am making some headway and I'm loving this cherry blossom fabric.

I wonder what Mika's fashions will look like. Now that Miss Melody approved both of our design drawings (which looked really similar!!), I'm completely worried our actual fashion outfits will look the same. I want my creations to be unique and fabulous, not the same as Meanie Mika's! And I so do not want to work on that banner with Mika on Monday.

Ugh, one more day of worrying left to go. I usually love Miss Melody's ideas, but this working-together idea is not a winner.

Off to our Cupcake Catch-Up . . . TTYL!

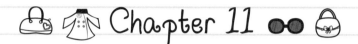

Chapter 11

Sew Long Sunday

Sunday

So Dad tried to help me on the sewing machine today . . .

Look how that turned out:

I told him I was hungry for one of his delicious egg omelets. <u>Anything</u> to get him away from my designs!

FACT Dad = **DEFINITELY NOT** creative.
(SORRY, DAD!)

Yesterday, at CCU, the girls and I talked about my annoying banner project. I am <u>so</u> not looking forward to recess tomorrow! Coco tried to cheer me up with her latest cupcake recipe: caramel chocolate-chip cupcakes with chocolate frosting. YUM!

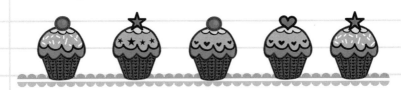

While we were decorating our yummy creations, Coco and Lulu filled me in on how their art projects were coming along. . . .

Coco's doing a portrait of Evie that looks amazing. I wish I could paint like she does.

Lulu's pottery is almost finished. She made three vases and a money box. She plans to sell the vases and keep the money box (to hold her newfound cash!).

Okay, well, back to my sewing machine. Then off to bed. Not that there will be much sleeping happening tonight . . . ☹

Chapter 12

Best Friends Are the Bestest

Monday

BANNER SCHMANNER! Today I honestly tried to be friendly with Mika. I was even doing ALL the drawings for the banner. (Mika was doing the writing.) But Mika was SO completely rude. Check out these two drawings I made:

Then check out what happened next....

"I've drawn 2 pictures for our banner. Which looks better, the lotus flower or the cat?" — me

"Which one's the cat?" — Mika

"This one. See the whiskers?" — me

"Oh, I thought that one was a fish." — Mika

(It looks NOTHING like a fish!)

"Did I ask you if you liked the lotus flower or the fish?" — me

"No. That's why I thought it was weird you drew a fish." — Mika

(??!!#%)

"It's not a fish." — me

"Well, why does it have whiskers?" — Mika

"Because it's a cat, not a fish!" — me

"A catfish?" — Mika

(She thinks she's so clever! She even sort of smiled at me!)

"Whatever. Do you like the lotus flower better, then?" — me

"Which one is the lotus flower?" — Mika

"Okay, I think we're done." — me

The recess bell rang just in time. Miss Melody said our banner would have to do since it needs to be hung up today. PHEW!

FASHION PARADE
THIS WEDNESDAY

After school, Coco and Lulu came over for Super Scrapbooking. We decided to use the time to work on our art projects instead of scrapbooking, though. That's when the doorbell rang.

You're not going to believe who it was — Mika!! She said she wanted to apologize for the fish/cat "misunderstanding." I couldn't believe it. Was she being friendly?? Then Dad invited her in!

Well, you won't believe it, but we all actually kind of, sort of had fun together. And Mika is really good at sewing. Everything was going well. That is until Coco and Lulu tried on my kimono fashions. They're my models, remember?

Then Mika said this:

"Maybe those kimonos would look better on Maxi?" — Mika

I could not believe she said that! Mika is SOOOO completely rude! Coco and Lulu got really upset. Here's what happened next:

"Are you saying Maxi is better looking than we are?" — **Coco**

"Are you saying we look like <u>dogs</u>?" — **Lulu**

"Uh, no, I wasn't saying that exactly . . . Maxi would just look . . . " — **Mika**

"That's it, Mika! Coco and Lulu are beautiful!! At least I have friends who <u>want to model</u> my clothes! Who do you have?! Maxi should be <u>your</u> model since <u>no person</u> would ever agree to help someone as mean as you!" — me

I was this angry:

Mika turned red. Then she looked my dog up and down, and stormed out of my house.

Coco, Lulu, and I just looked at each other. Then we quietly went back to work. I guess we all knew what I'd just said was pretty mean. But, really, Mika was being soooo mean, too!!

I'm almost finished sewing my fashions for the parade. I've just got a few finishing touches to add tomorrow night. I cannot believe the fashion parade is the day after tomorrow! EEK!
Good night, Diary.

Chapter 13

VP
of
Drama

Tuesday

Mika is UNBELIEVABLE!! She kept trying to talk
to me in class today! I mostly just ignored her.
I didn't want to get into another cat or dog
fight with her, especially not the day before the
BIG fashion parade. She kept saying, "But I just
want to borrow . . ." As if!!!
As if I would lend her anything after what she
said yesterday!

After school was fun (thanks to the LLGC!).
We had Doggie Day Spa at Coco's house.
Maxi loved it! I could tell because he was
wagging his tail so much.

Then Coco's mom invited Lulu and me to stay
at their house for dinner. Count me in! Their
food is always 500 times better than Dad's!

We ate spaghetti with a funny green sauce on it. Mrs. Corvino called it "pesto sauce" but I call it **delicioso**! (AND it's not eggs, so that makes it doubly delicious!)

Lulu walked home with me after dinner (two doors down) with Maxi and Bosco by our sides. Then she and Bosco went to her house.

DELICIOSO= Italian for "delicious"

My stomach is filled with butterflies about
tomorrow, but it sure felt good to be with my
Lotus Lane Girls tonight. I'm in bed now.
Good night, Diary.

✤ ✤ Chapter 14 ✤ ✤

Who Let the Dog Out?

Wednesday

OH NO!!!!!!!!

Maxi is missing! I can't remember if I shut the gate last night or not. (I haven't told Dad this....) I was so busy talking to Lulu on the walk home that I can't remember. What if this is ALL MY FAULT??? What if Maxi went to dig in Mika's sand again? What if Mika called the dogcatcher just like she said she would!?!

I'm so sad and worried. Dad and I looked everywhere for Maxi. Now I don't even care about today's fashion parade (well, not really, but you know what I mean). I just want Maxi back.

Have to go to school.

EEK! 20 minutes until the fashion parade starts. Maxi is STILL missing. Dad said he'd text me as soon as he hears anything. No texts. ☹

OH MY GOODNESS!

EEK times 1,000,000!!!! Diary, you will never in a trillion years guess what happened today!!!!!!

At the fashion parade, Mika's designs went on first. And guess who came out onstage to model them . . .

Yup, onstage . . . in a doggie-sized kimono!!
Maxi and Mika's Great Dane, Bob, were modeling Mika's fashions!

I was stunned — as was the rest of the school. Of course, I was <u>BEYOND HAPPY</u> to see Maxi. I just couldn't believe Mika was now also a <u>DOG-NAPPER</u>! I looked over at Mika and she actually <u>SMILED</u> back at me. A really big smile. I couldn't believe her!!

Mika's "models" left the stage. Then Coco and Lulu went on to model my designs. I was feeling sooo angry at Mika and sooo nervous about my designs. But then I looked out at the audience and saw Mom standing in the back! What a great surprise!! And everyone was clapping for my designs! ☺

After Coco and Lulu went offstage, Mika came up to me.

FACT Mika is someone who takes things (and says things!) quite exactly.

Mika said, "Remember how you told me 'Maxi should be your model'?" She said that what I said about Maxi inspired her to change her designs at the last minute. It turns out she didn't want our designs to look the same either. And she thought I was giving her permission to borrow Maxi for the fashion parade!! She said she tried to ask me for sure yesterday (but I was ignoring her because of the dog fight).

Mika told me she had only said the kimonos would look better on Maxi (than on Coco and Lulu), because she had doggie fashions on her mind. (Maybe my chickens will be next!)

Mika said she saw our gate open when she woke up today. She figured I had left it open so she could borrow Maxi. (I guess I should just be thankful Maxi wasn't stolen by someone FOR REAL. And maybe I should apologize to Dad for leaving the gate open again.)

Sorry, Dad.

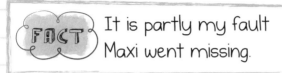

FACT It is partly my fault Maxi went missing.

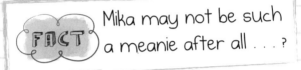

FACT Mika may not be such a meanie after all . . . ?

After the parade, Mika said she liked my fashions. Oh, and we both won awards!!!! I think Miss Melody thinks we must have worked together. . . .

When you're really creative like me (and Mika!), sometimes your imagination can run wild — like how mine came up with Meanie Mika: the giant-ant-owning, evil fashion copycat, and mastermind dog-napper! OOPSY.

I couldn't have won this award without my Lotus Lane BFFs! Coco and Lulu are the BEST!

Oh, and they won awards for their art passion projects, too. Coco won the Most Lifelike Art award and Lulu won the Most Useful Art award.

Coco's Painting

Lulu's Vase

I hugged Maxi and then ran to see Mom and Dad. I was so happy Mom made it to my fashion parade! Tomorrow, I'm going to tell her what happened while she was away.

Good thing I told you **EVERYTHING**, Diary!!

Okay, time to go celebrate with my Lotus Lane Girls!

Thanks for listening. **BYE!**

Love,
Kiki

Kyla May

lives near the beach in
Australia with her husband,
three daughters, two dogs,
two cats, and four guinea pigs.

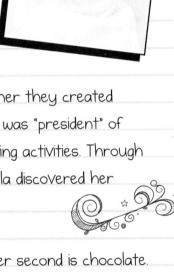

Growing up, Kyla lived on a
close-knit tree-lined avenue.
This is where she met her
childhood best friends (who are
still her dearest friends!). Together they created
their own girls club, where Kyla was "president" of
sticker collecting and roller-skating activities. Through
these childhood best friends, Kyla discovered her
endless imagination.

Kyla's first passion is drawing. Her second is chocolate.

HOW MUCH DO YOU KNOW ABOUT ?

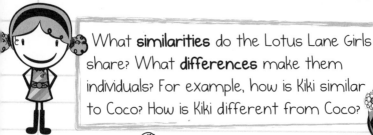

What **similarities** do the Lotus Lane Girls share? What **differences** make them individuals? For example, how is Kiki similar to Coco? How is Kiki different from Coco?

Why does Miss Melody say Kiki and Mika are on "the same creative page"? Reread Chapter 9 to find clues in the text and in the art.

How does Kiki react when Mika says that Kiki's kimono fashions might look better on Maxi than on Coco and Lulu? Do you think Kiki handled the situation well? Why or why not?

How is Kiki's diary **similar to** and **different from** other diary-like books you have read?

Write your own diary entries. Use **text** and **art** to include all the events that have happened in the past few days.